Dead On Its Tracks

More **Strange Matter**™ from
Marty M. Engle & Johnny Ray Barnes, Jr.

Dead On Its Tracks

Johnny Ray Barnes Jr.

**A
MONTAGE
PUBLICATION**

Montage Publications, a Front Line company,
San Diego, California

ISBN 1-56714-047-5

Printed in the U.S.A.

TO OUR FAMILY AND FRIENDS

(YOU KNOW WHO YOU ARE.)

1

The morbid anticipation of being afraid, of knowing that unforgettable horrors awaited me just ahead, filled my mind with images of grotesque, man-eating things that promised to haunt my dreams that very night.

But I wouldn't have it any other way.

When I saw a good horror movie, a really good horror movie, I had nightmares. If I made those kind of films, I'd want to give kids bad dreams. It's better than applause. It's better than a good review. It means you really scared them.

That's the effect I hoped "Terror Train" would have on me. The movie, a story of zombies invading a train, had been called the scariest since "Jaws", and I had to see it to believe it. After a week's worth of begging and pleading (a

PG movie that critics said would keep the whole family up nights, even the dog!), Mom and Dad finally gave the nod to let me go.

"Elizabeth, when do I need to pick you up?" Mom asked, turning the corner of Forest Drive, and bringing Fairfield's Gideon 8 Theatres into full view.

"Two hours, Mom," I answered. "You can't ever go wrong with two hours. You're either just a little early or a little late."

"Besides, I don't think her attention span could handle anything much longer than that," my friend, Jacob, smart-mouthed, instantly receiving my elbow in his ribs for his trouble.

"Elizabeth Martin, calm down," Mom commanded as we rolled into the parking lot.

Staying calm was tough when Jacob and I got together. I think his weirdness is contagious. When he's not around, I'm pretty normal. Well, as normal as a football, baseball, basketball-playing girl can be. Everyone calls me a tomboy, except for Jacob. He just says, 'You're scary, man,' then rattles off some kind of story or joke he has dancing in his head. The kids at school think we're a couple, but we're just buddies with a lot in common.

2

Like horror movies. We both *love* them.

"I hope it's a good one. Nothing's scared me since that blackout a couple of months ago," Jacob admitted.

"Well, I saw an episode of 'Night Gallery' that creeped me out bad. This girl found a monster trapped in a pit, and she began to visit it everyday . . ." My words died off as the car stopped at the front entrance.

"Two hours, then," Mom said as we opened our doors and hopped out. "And be here up front where the lights are. It'll be dark by then."

"No problem-o, Mom-o," I said into the car before shutting the door and bounding over to the ticket window.

Few things are better than going to the movies. Hitting a pitch over the fence, maybe. Or out-running that guy who, for a month, has been teasing you to race him. But other than things like that, there's nothing as rewarding as viewing a movie you've been dying to see on the big screen.

For Jacob and me, Terror Train had been a long time coming. He'd primed me for it, telling me the real-life horror stories the movie had been based on. It sounded too good to miss, and today we'd finally get to see it.

We both dug our money out from our pockets, walking up that red-carpeted ramp to the ticket window. The usher moved into stub-ripping position. The concession attendant set up two cups in hopes of filling them. The ticket cashier reached above her head, placing something directly over our movie's title on the listing board.

We came to a stop.

No way. No stinking way.

Sold out?

NO.

A total and complete injustice.

A stinging slap to the face.

I unsteadily made my way up to the counter, my brows furrowed in confusion.

"Terror Train? Sold out?" I asked.

"Sold out," answered the cashier. "But we still have seats for our seven o'clock show."

"I have a game tonight. I can't make the seven o'clock show," I told her. "Couldn't you let us in? We'll sit in the aisles if we have to."

"Sorry," she said. "It's against fire code regulations."

"This can't be happening . . ." I muttered to myself as Jacob leaned up to the ticket window.

"Can I at least get some mints?" he asked.

Jacob crammed his mouth full of Junior Mints as we walked back out in front of the theatre.

"I guess I'll call my mom to come pick us up, if she's even home yet. This stinks," I griped. "Why couldn't they show it in two theatres?"

"We could always go see another movie," Jacob said, pulling one huge mint made up of ten globbed-together little ones from his candy box. Obviously he had decided to make the best of the situation.

"Forget it. I'm not going to see an action movie. I'm sick of action movies. And I don't want to see one of those stupid cyber-thrillers either," I told him.

Jacob smiled as he chewed the wad of chocolate that was almost too big for his mouth. Behind his eyes, a light bulb glowed brighter with every munch.

"What? What is it?" I asked.

He finished chomping, wiping the excess

candy from his lips with the back of his hand.

"Well, do you still want to see something scary?" he asked slyly.

"What are you talking about?" I asked him, giggling just a bit at his serious attitude.

He kept staring at me with his stony expression until I became uneasy, and stopped laughing.

"What is it, Jacob?" I asked again.

Then he cracked a smile.

"I know where we can find something scarier than that movie," he said. "I know where we can find a *real* Terror Train."

"What are you talking about?" I asked him.

"What I'm talking about," Jacob said as he leaned in closer, "is the Fairfield Express."

The Fairfield Express? He had to be pulling my leg. Everyone in town had seen the Fairfield Express pictured in the Gazette only two weeks before. It's a steam engine, nothing more than a tourist gimmick. The train runs on an old track that circles the town. On the way, the passengers get to listen to the train conductor go on about Fairfield history, and the train makes a couple of stops at historical sights. It also costs six dollars a person. What a rip-off!

"Okay, I'm calling my mom to pick us up," I said, blowing the whole thing off as a joke.

Jacob stopped me. "No, no. Don't. I'm serious. You may think I'm kidding, but there's a lot about that train that people don't know."

"So what's so scary about it?" I decided to give him one more chance to convince me.

"I'll tell you . . . on the way." He backed up like he had just handed me a lit firecracker.

"On the way where?" I asked, even though I knew the answer. "We're not going to see the Fairfield Express. My mom's picking us up soon."

"She's not picking us up for two hours. It'll only take us thirty minutes to get there and back. Come on. Be adventurous!" Jacob backed up to the edge of the sidewalk, motioning me to come along. "Thirty minutes, Elizabeth. That's all it will take."

"Then what? Come back here and hang out for an hour and a half?" I asked, picking at the details of his idea.

"Yes. If we go, I'll gladly come back here with you and hang out for an hour and a half," Jacob promised.

I bit my lip, calculating the trouble factor. Then I looked over at the attractions window in front of the theatre doors. The Terror Train poster taunted me with its dripping title and the ever-so-frightening zombie engineer steering the locomotive straight to death's door. Oh, how I wanted to see that movie.

"All right, let's go see it," I said. If I couldn't see my movie, I'd see the next best thing. I hoped.

Jacob gave a low, sneaky chuckle, then turned around to make sure no cars were coming down either side of the street. As soon as he ran across, I followed.

When we reached the other side, I asked, "So what's the story? What's so terrifying about the Fairfield Express?"

"Well, my dad told me all about it, without my mom knowing, of course. She doesn't like him telling me scary stories. But I've got to warn you, what makes this story so terrifying, so utterly and unimaginably horrifying, is that everything in it . . . is the truth."

Jacob had my complete and total attention. All of the sounds around us seemed to disappear into the background as his tale unfolded.

"It all happened back in 1878. The steam engine that we call the Fairfield Express was about twenty years old then. And on every one of the days in every one of those years, the same man had been the engineer on the train, up until two weeks prior to the accident."

"What accident?" I asked.

"Just wait. I'll get to that. Anyway, the engineer's name was John Cape. Everyone called him Odd John because after years of railroading, he started going a little crazy."

"A little crazy?" I wondered aloud.

"Shhh. Yeah, crazy. He spent every second he could on the train. He didn't like being off of it. He ate all his meals in the dining car. He slept in one of the passenger cars every night. They say he never left the tracks because he knew exactly where they went. Leaving them to wander aimlessly about in a town or the countryside scared him to death. So he lived on the train, and considered it his one and only home.

When the railroad tried to work on the engine and repair parts of it, Odd John went crazy, threatening to shoot anyone who touched his home. After that, the railroad forced him to retire. He moved into a shack just outside of town, right next to the train tracks, of course, and never left."

"That doesn't explain the accident," I said.

"It will. You see, the railroad hired a new engineer, and moved him here from France."

"From France?" I asked.

"Hey, he was a good engineer. Pierre Deschaul, the first Deschaul to come to Fairfield, and the first Deschaul to succumb to its cold and flu season."

"You mean . . ."

"On what was probably one of the most important trips in that steam engine's history, Pierre Deschaul was bedridden, and the train

11

didn't have an engineer. That's when the Mayor of Fairfield at the time, Donald M. Ledger himself, got into the picture. You see, his daughter was sick, too. A lot sicker than Pierre. So sick she had to be rushed by train to a hospital up in the big city. With no other options, Mayor Ledger reinstated Odd John Cape immediately."

"Bad move," I said.

"Well, yeah. But the Mayor was so desperate, he didn't care how crazy Odd John was, as long as he could drive the train. How could he have known that days of sitting in his shack, watching his beloved train steam right past him had driven poor Odd John completely insane? Anyway, Odd John climbed into the engine with every intention of making that the last trip for everyone on-board."

Jacob stopped talking, paused for a moment, and then continued, "The Mayor had made the trip to the big city numerous times. He knew exactly how long it took, how many farms they passed along the way, and how fast the train took certain turns. When it rounded the curve just before Sutter's Pass, which is about twenty-five miles out of town, Donald M. Ledger knew they were going too fast."

"What did he do?"

"He pulled for the brake, but the lines had been cut. When he got up to check on things, the train lurched around the next turn, knocking people into each other. Everyone in the passenger cars began to panic, screaming and running for the doors. Mayor Ledger realized his fatal mistake. He ran to the very first passenger car and yanked open its front door. Even through the noise of the pistons and spinning wheels, the Mayor could hear Odd John Cape laughing. A laugh so maniacal, it would chill you in your grave. As they crossed Sutter's Pass, the Mayor knew he had doomed the whole train."

"Why? What happened?" I asked.

"Just beyond Sutter's Pass, there's a great drop-off to the Cutooga River. As they crossed the pass, the train was going faster than any train the Mayor had ever seen. They flew off the tracks, and went over the edge. Everyone screamed with their very last breaths except for Odd John Cape. They say he laughed all the way down."

"And the Fairfield Express? It's the same train?" I couldn't believe there would have been much left of it.

"For the most part. See, the passenger and freight cars were demolished. But what's really weird is that the engine came out of the wreck almost completely intact. It's been repaired and restored over the years, but some say the spirit of Odd John still rides the helm of the engine to this day."

Within fifteen minutes of leaving the theatre, we spotted the Fairfield Train Depot from the hilltop.

At the moment, a train was leaving the station. Jacob and I watched the diesel train make its way from the stop, and slowly accelerate down the tracks. A few people milled about in and around the depot, but no one looked exceptionally busy.

"Hmmm. Day to day goings on at the railroad station. Pretty exciting stuff," I said snidely.

"Oh yeah? Well, there's the Fairfield Express, smarty," he shot back, pointing to a separate track a few yards a way.

It looked like a classic 'choo-choo' train. One engine and two passenger cars, painted red with yellow trim. In circus lettering on the sides, it said 'The Fairfield Express'.

"That looks *really spooky*," I kidded some more.

"Well, let's go over there and take a look at it." Jacob started down the small hill we stood on, heading for the tracks.

"HEY, WAIT!" I commanded. "We can't go over there. We'll get in trouble!"

Jacob kept moving, burying his hands in his pockets and keeping his head down.

I looked at the depot. No one seemed to be making any kind of fuss. I hadn't been to many train depots, but I didn't think they wanted kids wandering over the tracks. I felt certain that at any second someone would run out there and grab him.

But it never happened. Jacob walked across the tracks, and finally came to a stop on the other side of the Fairfield Express. He looked my way, grinned, then motioned for me to follow.

Well, if he made it, I could. And faster, too. I took one quick glance over at the depot building, then took off. I sprinted across the tracks, not looking over my shoulder for a second. I came to a screeching halt beside Jacob, and he pulled me to the side of the train.

"What are you worried about?" Jacob whispered. "Do you think we're the first kids who ever ran across the railroad tracks? It's practically a Fairfield tradition."

"Just get all the way behind the engine before someone sees us," I snapped.

Then I heard voices.

"I'm telling you," said the one of the voices, "I saw someone around the train."

I froze in terror.

We were caught.

"Seriously, last night, someone moved inside the train," came the voice again.

Jacob and I had stopped in our tracks and crouched down, just out of sight of the two men who stood on the platform right over us. Every bone in my body wanted to shake out of my skin, but I gripped Jacob's arm and held myself together.

"Well, Rupert, do you think we have vandals sneaking on the train at night?" asked the other man.

"I don't know. There was nothing messed up in any of the cars. But who knows how many nights this has been going on? If I hadn't forgotten some tools I needed last night, I never would've come back here and seen them," explained Rupert.

I remembered reading in the Gazette article that Rupert Mulligan worked on the Fairfield Express as Head Engineer. He is responsible for making sure the train is in tip-top shape.

"Well, do you think we should put someone out here to watch things at night?" asked the other man.

"Maybe that would be good. I lock up the cars every night, though. I can't figure out how they could've gotten in," Rupert said, his foot kicking dirt off the end of the platform. It sprinkled on our heads. Rupert had stepped to the edge to look closer at something. He leaned over, just above us, to gaze at a passenger window.

Jacob and I didn't breathe. If Rupert looked down, we'd be caught.

He wiped his hand over something on the window. "Someone's been in there, all right. Must've breathed on the window and then drew on it with their finger. It says 'HELP'," Rupert announced.

Then he stepped back on the dock.

He hadn't seen us.

My heart slid from my throat back into my chest.

"Well, let's go into the Depot and I'll give ol'

Ivan Brewer a call and see if he can cut his vacation short. He'll keep an eye on the train for us," said the other man, who by now I guessed must be Mr. Davenport, the Depot Director who was also mentioned in the article.

Their footsteps led off into the distance, and I finally took a breath. So did Jacob. I saw his face turn from blue, to red, and then back to normal.

"Let's get out of here," I whispered.

"Let's see inside the train first," Jacob answered.

I wanted to tear off his head, clean all the dumb stuff out and then slap it back on. "You are completely insane. Those two men can't be far away. They'll catch us!"

"Come on," he said, and then made his way to the passenger car steps, grabbed the handles and climbed on-board.

"I'm going to regret this," I muttered to myself, then followed him up.

I'd never seen a passenger car like this one.

We walked down a narrow hall, with three different doors to our left. I marveled at the finished wood paneling on the walls, running my fingers across it to feel its slickness. The windows looked clear, not a speck of dirt on them. I strained my eyes to see my own reflection. My feet kneaded their way into the fine, soft carpeting beneath me. Its paisley design made me think of a shirt hanging in my dad's closet that he never wore.

I'd ridden on an Amtrak train once to visit my uncle and aunt. This passenger car may have been older, but it out-classed the new ones a hundred-fold.

"What do you think?" Jacob whispered.

"What's in there?" I asked, pointing to the

center door. Now that we'd snuck on, I wanted to see everything.

Jacob fingered the latch and slid the door to the side.

"Wow," he remarked.

Plush, floral design upholstery covered three separate sets of seats inside the compartment. Jacob walked inside, instantly plopping down on the biggest cushion.

"Ahh. This is the life. Get me a sandwich. And some milk please," he commanded, sliding further and further into his seat.

"Get a life. And some brains," I said, reaching over his head to switch on a wall lamp that drooped above him like a dead tulip. Light filled the compartment and brought dots to my eyes.

"AAAAGGgghhh," I cried.

"Very bright of you," Jacob quipped, but then shouted, "ELIZABETH, GET DOWN!"

With a vise-like grip on my arm, he pulled me to the floor. When my vision cleared a bit, I saw Jacob turning off the light, and then diving to the floor beside me.

"What is it?" I saw the look on his face and knew the news wouldn't be good.

"It's Rupert. He came back out. I think he's

coming in the car!" Jacob exclaimed softly.

In one synchronized move, he looked to his left and I to my right. The seats had ample room under them for someone of our size to hide. Again at the same time, we rolled beneath the furniture, he on one side of the compartment and I on the other.

We stopped moving just as Rupert came through the door.

"I knew it," he mumbled to himself. "I keep all these compartment doors closed. Some delinquent is sneaking on my train." He walked over to the window. I heard him spit, then wipe the window. "There. No more 'HELP'", he muttered. "I'd like to see the brats who did this get on this train tonight!" With that, he left the compartment, sliding the door shut behind himself.

Jacob and I stared at each other while we listened for him to leave. We heard some clanking noises, but couldn't be sure if he had actually left the train or not.

Then we heard Mr. Davenport's voice again, catching Rupert just outside the train. They struck up another conversation, but this one sounded muffled, too difficult to hear. But as long as they stood out there, we'd stay put.

I looked at my watch. Forty minutes had passed since we left the theatre. Signaling Jacob, I pointed to my watch.

He shrugged.

I made a mental note to rake him over the coals later. If my mom came to the theatre and couldn't find us, she'd put everyone who even thought about becoming a policeman on the streets looking for us. And where would they would find us? On the Fairfield Express! Punishment would reach a new level with Mom's swift disciplinary action.

Rupert and Mr. Davenport seemed to go on forever. I rolled out from under the seat to keep my arms and legs from going numb. I soon noticed Jacob actually dozing. The sun sank lower and lower in the sky.

Then, very unexpectedly, the conversation just ended. The two men headed off in different directions, with Mr. Davenport yelling back to Rupert, "Ivan will be here in an hour, so go on home!"

I waited in complete silence for a few more seconds before I grabbed Jacob's leg, scaring him so badly that he shot up and smacked his head against the bottom of the seat.

"Oooowwww! Ow, momma!" he cried out.

"Come on, let's get out of here! We've only got an hour and ten minutes!" I pulled him out by the shirt with one hand, and reached for the compartment door with the other. We both got to our feet as I slapped the compartment door open, then hustled through the corridor to the closed car door.

I grabbed the handle and pulled.

To my horror, I saw a padlocked chain jerk into the air on the other side.

Rupert had done it.

He'd locked us in.

"**NOOO!**" I wailed. "**NOOOO!**"

Jacob seized my arms as they jerked at the doors.

"**CHILL!** There's probably another way out!" He turned and took off back down the corridor. Before I could get to him, I heard the same lurching motion I'd just made up front. "**RATS!**" Jacob yelled.

"What about the roof?" I scanned the ceiling for an opening. Nothing.

"Nothing there or the floor," said Jacob, pacing the corridor and losing his cool. "Let's break a window."

"No way! You remember how Bloody Ben Blumer got his nickname? We'll be cut to ribbons!" I tried to keep my mind focused. If I didn't, I would've jumped on Jacob and strangled him.

He stopped his fluttering about and gave in to our last option. "I guess we might as well start screaming! **HELP! SOMEBODY HELP US!**"

"RRRRR," I growled, and pounced on Jacob. I pinned his shoulders to the floor, which shut him up pretty quick. "The sun's setting Jacob! When we get in trouble for this, who's going to tell my mom it was their idea?"

"M-me," Jacob squeaked.

"And when I miss my baseball game tonight, who's going to tell my coach how I got locked in a train because of a certain lunk-headed idea?"

"Me," he said, squirming.

The light was fading fast in the passenger car, leaving just enough illumination on Jacob's face to reveal his apologetic expression.

"You better," I told him, just as the entire passenger car started making noise. A broken chorus of creaking and clanking, like the whole car was preparing to fall apart. It started low at first, but then grew increasingly louder.

We both jumped to our feet, looking out the windows for an answer.

Nothing out there.

Then the car lurched forward.

Jacob fell backwards onto the floor, but I

grabbed hold of the window sill.

Looking out the window again, I noticed the ground beginning to move.

"Jacob," I yelled. **"WE'RE MOVING!"**

Jacob shot up to the window.

"WE'RE MOVING DOWN THE TRACK! HOW ARE WE DOING THAT?"

Running over to the door, I jerked at it continuously with all my might, trying to loosen the chain enough to open it.

Suddenly, the handle became unbearably hot.

"ARRGGHH! MY HANDS!" The heat practically burned them before I could let go. Smoke came from the door as if a fire blazed on the other side. But I didn't see anything through the window. No light at all! "JACOB, SOMETHING'S ON FIRE! BUT I CAN'T SEE IT!"

The train picked up speed, and Jacob and I continued running back and forth in the passenger car, trying to open windows and doors in time to jump out before the train got moving too fast. The heat rippled over the floor, and the smothering air grew thicker in the compartment, making it hard to breathe.

I'd had enough.

Cutting myself on a couple of pieces of glass would be nothing compared to being roasted alive. Dashing into the compartment we had hidden in, I braced my foot against a seat, pulled the lamp from the wall, and launched it at the window. It exploded like an eggshell against a brick wall, and glass shattered all over the compartment.

"IT WON'T WORK!" Jacob yelled. "I TRIED IN THE OTHER COMPARTMENT! THESE WINDOWS ARE TOO STRONG!"

"WHAT ARE WE GOING TO DO?" I screamed, sweat pouring from my forehead. The entire car had become a sauna.

Then I noticed something outside, pouring off the train.

Something red.

"Is . . . is that blood?" I asked.

We rushed to the window as a rain of red poured from the train, covering the window with a thick, lumpy coat.

"There's something else mixed in with it," Jacob noticed. "Another color."

"Yellow?" I asked myself out loud. Yes, yellow. *The paint.* The red and yellow paint that covered the train! Looking down at the sill on the outside of the train, I saw the paint bubble up, then blow off in drops. Underneath it lay dark, scarred metal that looked a hundred years old. "It's the heat. It's melting the paint away!"

"ELIZABETH! LOOK!" Jacob yelled.

Whipping around, I instantly felt a shock. I expected to see the mess I'd made on the floor with the lamp.

But it wasn't there. Disappeared. *The whole train seemed to be changing!*

Suddenly, a flickering light danced on the walls in the corridor. From the compartment, I could see its reflection growing larger on the polished wood paneling, coming closer.

And I heard it crackle.

"FIRE!" I yelled, and just as I did, the flames jumped into the room.

"UP ON THE SEATS!" Jacob cried, and leaped up on the nearest one.

One single, small wall of flame ran across the carpet, scorching it to a black crust. It moved

31

as if it had a mission.

Before it climbed to the furniture, we jumped to the smoking, charred floor. The insides of the furniture burst open, filling the air with floating cotton.

The entire corridor had been burnt, roasted to a crusty, smoking black. We made our way to the door, hoping that the fire had somehow melted the chains. No luck. They still looked like new, and so did the lock.

We crouched in the corner, waiting for some miracle to happen before the flames leaped around the bend and fried us.

"I . . . I don't hear the fire," Jacob said.

I got up, looked around the corner, and saw nothing but scorched passenger car. Carefully, I peeked into the compartment where we'd been. The fire was gone.

Jacob came up behind me. "What's going on?"

Suddenly, we heard the train whistle go off, and at the front of the car, the door connecting us with the steam engine slowly slid open.

At first, we breathed a sigh of relief. The cool wind that blew into the passenger car revitalized us, carrying much needed air to our lungs and brains. But that soon gave way to chilling questions of what had opened that door, and what drove the train?

The noise from the locomotive just beyond the doorway pounded inside my head. It sounded evil, leading me to imagine a giant beast waiting for me right outside the door. *Or a zombie,* a scene straight from the preview of Terror Train. I rationalized that maybe, and it would be the only reason to walk through that door, but maybe, we could somehow stop the train. A long shot, but I couldn't see any other options. If we tried to jump off, we'd break our necks.

I made the first step, and Jacob followed

closely behind me. The gusts that blew in now alternated between hot and cold, sending my body into an uncentralized shiver as I approached the doorway. The steam that curled around the opening made it impossible to see through to the engine, and as I stepped through, it occurred to me that there might not be anything out there at all.

But there was. The train coupling. And just beyond it, the tender. The tender housed the coal and water used by the train. We'd have to go around it, then come up to the engineer's cab. Once we circled this, and gone maybe two small steps up to the cab, the identity of our mystery engineer would be revealed.

"Go on . . ." Jacob whispered. He still stood inside the passenger car behind me. I reached in, grabbed his shirt, and pulled him through. The door shut tight just as he cleared it, and then we lost all sound.

I moved my head around, trying to determine if my ears had gone out. But when I saw the confusion on Jacob's face, too, I knew something had happened. The train was deathly silent, but still forged ahead, going faster than Rupert probably ever intended it to.

"Elizabeth . . . " Jacob said. I heard his voice, and he sounded scared out of his wits.

He pointed past me, toward the engine.

Silhouetted by the steam, walked a thin figure of a person, slowly moving around the tender to the engine.

I froze. If we moved forward, he could be waiting there to grab us. Who knew what he'd do?

"Maybe it's Rupert," whispered Jacob.

"Not fat enough," I said, looking down for something, anything, to protect myself with if that guy jumped out of nowhere. Finding an old charred stick that had probably been used for spreading coal, I held it in a tight grip close to my side, and moved forward.

I chose to round the tender on the side opposite the man, the left side. My senses felt all out of whack, with so much motion going on around me, but not a single sound coming from any of it. If the mysterious figure sneaked up behind us, I'd never hear him. As we rounded the turn at the front of the tender, I stopped immediately, letting Jacob bump into me from behind.

With my head, I motioned to the engine.

The figure, still obscured by the steam, stood

in the engineer's cab, shoveling loads of coal into the firebox at a frantic rate. The coal would go into the boiler, producing more steam, which would make the train go faster. *He wanted to go faster?*

"This is insane," I whispered to Jacob. "He's got to stop this train, now. I bet he doesn't even know he had a fire on-board."

"How are we going to stop him?" asked Jacob.

"We'll ask him first," I said. "And if that doesn't work, I'll use this." I slapped the heavy stick in my palm, making a whapping sound.

With Jacob behind me, I walked up to the engineer's cab.

The figure worked furiously, scooping load after load of black rock and flinging it into the locomotive's belly. He was dressed in engineer's clothing, with a bandanna tied over the bottom of his face. Then, with its back to me, the figure leaned over to adjust the throttle control, and I took my chance . . .

"PLEASE, SIR. STOP THIS TRAIN NOW!" I yelled.

The figure froze, then slowly turned around. With its gloved hand, it removed the bandanna from its face . . .

REVEALING A HUMAN SKULL.

I shrieked in terror, dropping the stick and falling backwards down the steps.

Then, with a cackling laugh, the thing threw its shovel to the floor, looked down at me and spoke. "You can't get off yet, girlie. It's not your stop."

The wooden stick swung through the air, striking the monster in the stomach!

"GET AWAY FROM HER!" Jacob screamed, his face so pale it almost glowed in the dark.

"AHHH . . . PARTNERS," cracked the skeleton engineer, then jerked Jacob up by the shirt and held him in the air.

"NO!" I moved to get up, but the monster's foot pinned me up against the tender, holding both of us at his mercy at the same time.

"WE'RE TAKING A JOURNEY," he said. "A JOURNEY THAT ENDS IN DEATH FOR EVERYONE ON THIS TRAIN."

His foot grew heavier, pressing me so hard it forced the air from my lungs.

Jacob hung there, sobbing into the monster's face. His eyes burned like what could have possibly been lit lumps of coal crammed in his head. A speckled skin of soot covered his yellowed skull, and flakes of ash fell off of when he spoke.

"You are the only two who can stop it." His voice curdled, then he dropped Jacob beside me on the platform and removed his foot from my chest.

What did he mean? What did he want? My brain felt like concrete, but Jacob got a question out.

"Who . . .Who are you?" Jacob cried. "Why won't you stop the train and let us off?"

"Some people have heard of me. I'm John Cape. Odd John Cape," he announced. "And I've been dead for over a hundred years."

Odd John Cape! The insane engineer!

"RUN, JACOB!" I yelled, jumping to my feet. Odd John's gloved hand snatched my shirt, and I felt my feet leave the ground. When he turned me around to face his rotted head, I saw Jacob clutched in the other hand, hanging parallel to me.

I didn't want to look the monster in the face, and neither did Jacob, but Odd John held us there, close enough to smell his rotten breath.

"I know what people say about me. I know they think I wrecked this train. But I loved this train, do you hear me? And I'd never have run her off the tracks. Someone aboard sabotaged my train." His voice rasped. "I want you to find out who it was."

He didn't let us go. He kept us dangling in the air and waited on our next words.

"But . . . but you're dead," I braved. "Why do you care anymore?"

The two coals lodged in his eye sockets burned brighter. "Because my spirit, and the spirits of all of the passengers on the train, cannot rest until the killer is known!"

"Then . . . then *you're* haunting the t-t-train?" Jacob stammered.

"Yes. It's my thirst for revenge that creates the haunting. It's me who drags every spirit of every passenger back with me to relive that horror all over again in hopes of finding the saboteur. He took away from me the only thing I ever loved!"

"How do you know it's a he?" I asked.

Odd John snarled and tossed us back to the floor.

"I don't! I don't know a thing! And I can

never find out on my own. I am cursed to be the engineer and the engineer only. While reliving this nightmare, I cannot leave my post."

Jacob stiffened, preparing himself if his question angered Odd John. "What will happen to you if you leave your post?"

Odd John started up the steps back to the engine, but then turned. "The haunting will end, and I'll never get my revenge. The saboteur will go free." Moving back up to the firebox, he began shoveling in more coal.

I turned to Jacob, who seemed oddly more at ease. "What is it?" I asked.

"Did you hear him? If we push him off this train, the whole thing's over. The train will stop and we can go home." His eyes scanned mine for acceptance.

"You do that," I told him, then turned my gaze to Odd John, who lowered his head from the billowing smoke back down to us.

"Go now," he said. "Go back to the cars. Find the saboteur. Free our spirits, and you will be returned. But you must go now, because time is running out!"

"Time's running out?" I asked.

He leaned down and spoke directly into my

face. "I told you. We're reliving the wreck. In less than an hour, this train will have an accident at Sutter's Pass. It'll kill us all, the dead and the living. Find out who it is, or this whole train's DEAD ON ITS TRACKS!"

11

The gruesome engineer stepped back, signaling us to get to our feet.

"Where?" Jacob asked. "Where are we going?"

"Back to the car," Odd John said morbidly.

Jacob and I backed away, never taking our eyes from him until the steam obscured his form.

We crept back to the passenger car door, and for the first time I noticed its color. Charred black, not a dot of paint anywhere. All of the color had melted off, showing the crusty black metal underneath. We stopped right at the doorway, checking to see if Odd John had followed us back.

"I can't believe it. Odd John Cape," remarked Jacob. "And you know what? Besides the obvious, he seemed pretty normal to me."

"Be quiet. I'm trying to weigh our options,"

I snapped.

"Weigh our options? It's do or die, Elizabeth. What else it there?" Jacob had obviously bought the entire story.

"Listen, if all of this is true, then we're going to die. This train is going to crash. I'm trying to figure out the best way to jump off before that happens." I told him.

He looked down at the ground speeding by and his face wrinkled in disbelief. "You're nuts! There is no 'best way' to jump off this train, unless you listed them in order of endured pain. Then I guess crushed legs and a cracked skull would be the 'best way'."

"Oh, Jacob, when are you going to get a clue? He wants us to find a saboteur that doesn't exist. And do you know why he doesn't exist? It's because Odd John wrecked this train and his guilty spirit is what we're dealing with! And even if that's not true, then where are the people to investigate? You and I were both on this passenger car and there were *no other people!*"

That's when Odd John reappeared from out of the steam, standing like a statue in the blowing smoke, and staring right at us.

"The saboteur is real," he spoke.

"You . . . you heard us?" I asked.

"Why do you think I keep it silent out here? I assure you one of the passengers is a saboteur, and he's just beyond that door. Find him now, or we're all doomed." Then Odd John took off his glove and pointed at the door with his bony finger. The steam covered him again.

Jacob and I turned to the door, and with a knot in my throat, I slid it open.

What lay on the other side made the horror of Odd John pale in comparison.

12

Throughout the entire passenger car walked the dead.

To our horror, most did not look as old as Odd John Cape. They looked fresher. Especially the one just inside the door.

Its body seemed to be nothing but a skeleton with a few muscles here and there, dipped in dripping, black tar. The eyeballs in its head stuck out like ping pong balls with pupils on them, and its teeth shone pearly white. It wore clothes, very stylish ones, with a vest, pocket watch, and hat that tipped back when the thing drank from its glass.

At the other end, two shriveled, old women gazed out the corridor window. They looked and dressed like twins, wearing dusty pink dresses with white flowers on them. But that didn't take away from their hideous features; flapping, wrinkled skin that hung like blankets from their bones, and black, hollow holes where their eyes should be.

And lastly, I saw what looked like a little boy run through the car and into one of the seating compartments. It happened in a flash, but I couldn't help catching that something was wrong with his head. Much too large, and moving in places it *shouldn't*.

Suddenly at the other end of the car, the door slid open.

"TICKETS. GET YOUR TICKETS READY," called the ticket master, a head carried by a very tall, ghost-white zombie.

Tickets?

The dribbling, tar-covered skeleton beside us turned up his drink, letting it trickle through his chin and onto his vest. He looked a little embarrassed, but then asked us, "You kids without tickets? I wouldn't let Headley catch you. He'll sic ol' Mumfrey on ya, and *he'll* throw you off this train *one piece at a time*."

"What'll we do?" I asked.

"Duck into that center compartment, and I'll get ol' Headley's attention distracted elsewhere!"

"TICKETS!" Headley called again, stopping when the two old women pulled their tickets from their purses.

Jacob and I moved quickly, gliding over to the compartment door, sliding it open and slipping through, shutting it behind us.

Once inside, I almost screamed at what I saw.

Smoke, heavier than the steam outside drifted through the air of the compartment, filling every inch, every corner with its winding mass.

At its center, four pairs of flaring, red eyes stared at Jacob and me.

Jacob turned, caught some of the smoke in his lungs, and began coughing uncontrollably. My hand clenched his shoulder, signaling him to pay attention. I felt him tense up when he noticed our audience, and his coughs quickly died off.

Something banged on the door behind us.

"LET US IN. I'VE GOT TO CHECK YOUR TICKETS!"

Headley. My eyes widened, filling with tears from the smoke. We had no place to run.

"You kids got tickets?" One pair of eyes

asked. Jacob didn't move. I managed to shake my head.

"Get under the seats," the eyes said. "We'll take care of it."

Without missing a beat, I slid under the long couch and Jacob went for the shorter seat, just as we'd done earlier that day.

The door slid open. The smoke filtered out of the room, revealing the owners of the watchful eyes. Only two could be seen from where I lay, but I felt thankful.

Grinning on the seat above Jacob, sat a mass of flesh that resembled a human chocolate drop. Its body rounded at the bottom, and came to a point at the very top. Two thin arms protruded from its sides, and its useless legs flopped over the chair seat, suspended in front of Jacob's face. It had a smiling face, with the reddest lips I'd ever seen, and pointed little teeth. The eyes squinted to accommodate its perpetual grin, which would have made it look asleep if it didn't flail its arms and jiggle so.

The other creature didn't seem as impressive, especially since it had nothing in it. A flattened man, completely devoid of anything inside him. He looked deflated, which made it all the more eerie when he leaned forward as Headley and Mumfrey made their way inside.

"I'm telling you Headley, good sir, that this is not the drink I ordered!" a voice yelled into the room.

The tar-covered man. Trying to distract Headley, I thought. *But it didn't work.*

"Tell it to the bartender. I'm the ticket man," Headley called back, and then Mumfrey held the ticket-checking head out to question the creatures in the compartment. "And I suppose all of you big gamblers have your tickets?"

The creatures, who'd been smoking, put their cigars aside. By the looks of the cards on the floor, they'd been gambling, too.

"Don't make us sound so sordid, Headley," said the big, fat one. "We're just passing the time by playing some cards. Why don't you just relax? Take a load off."

"Shaddup and give me your tickets," Headley snapped, and the dead creatures handed over their slips to Mumfrey's outstretched hand, who then put them up to Headley's mouth. He bit down on them to check all four. "Good day, gentlemen," he said, and then Mumfrey carried him out the door.

"Later, Headley. Keep your chin up," chuckled the thin, insideless man, and the rest of the crew burst out in laughter.

Jacob and I stayed perfectly still, hoping they'd forget about us, but . . .

"I think it's time we meet our visitors," gurgled the slobbering, grinning flesh mass with teeth.

14

"Are . . . are you going to eat us?" Jacob asked.

"Get out here, kid," said one of the creatures unseen by me. "Both of ya."

We slowly rolled out, and sat up in the middle of the floor. The creatures leaned in, looking at us as if we came from another planet, but one they knew of.

I'd definitely had the best view from under the furniture. At least my creatures were only unpleasant looking. The other two positively creeped me out. One was a rotted green shade, with skin that reminded me of a log. The other's head had been wrapped in bandages, but large tufts of black hair stuck out through them, even where the face should've been. *Were the bandages holding it together?*

Taking the cigar out of his mouth, the green man asked, "Excuse me, but how'd you kids get on without tickets?"

"We kind of . . . stowed away," I said, sliding back to the door.

"Where are you going?" asked the filthy, fat one. "Are you scared? Do you think we'll eat you?"

"No," I lied.

"Well, your little friend certainly does. Why don't you tell him to calm down?" Drops of spit fell from the large, fleshy one's mouth as it hovered over Jacob, who backed up and came to a stop beside me.

"Jacob, calm down," I said softly.

The man with no filling took a puff of his cigar, and the insides of his cheeks touched each other as he inhaled. "We did something for you, now you do something for us. We're traveling boys, you see. We gamble here, we gamble there. The last town we were in, we gambled badly, and made a few enemies. We spent every cent we had just getting out of town. Do you kids have any money?"

"I've got ten dollars," I said.

"I've got seven-fifty," said Jacob. "I . . .

bought mints."

"Seventeen dollars and fifty cents? What are you kids, rich? Anyway, you join us in a hand of cards, and we'll let you go. *If you win,*" the thin man said through a puff of smoke.

"What if we . . . don't win?" I asked, my voice trembling.

"Then we get your money, *and we get to eat you!* Hey, we haven't chowed in two days. I'm trying to be fair."

"Here," I pulled the money from my pocket. "Just take what I have! Please!"

"That's not our way, little girl. Didn't you hear me? We're gamblers!" the thin man said, and then broke into a chuckle, followed by his crew.

That's when Jacob leaned up to look over the cards. "What are you playing? he asked.

"Blackjack, son. Do you know how to play?" asked the green man, chomping on his cigar and smiling wide enough to see his black teeth.

"Yeah, no problem," Jacob said.

"What?" I whispered into his ear. He had to be bluffing.

"It's cool, Elizabeth," he whispered back. "Do you remember when I explained to you that my dad told me the story of the Fairfield Express? Well, he told me while we were playing blackjack."

"You gamble with your dad?" I asked.

"No, we never play for anything. He just likes doing it to unwind. Dad says cards aren't relaxing when you're playing for something," Jacob explained.

"Kiddies, are you gonna talk all day or play cards?" asked the thin man, shutting Jacob and me up. "Okay, since you're putting your money together you can play the same hand."

With his flappy arm, the thin man dealt the cards. He definitely had a system down. The cards spun in the air, coming to land face down right in front of each player. With an extra twist of his wrist, they landed face up.

"Now, everybody look at what'cha got," he said after he'd thrown the last card to Jacob.

Jacob looked at his cards, and remained emotionless. I couldn't read him at all. "Well?" I asked him. "Are we going to win?"

"If our cards equal twenty-one in value without going over, yeah we'll win. Otherwise, we've got to come closer to twenty-one than anyone else," he explained.

"Well, we're pretty close," I said, adding our two cards up to equal seventeen.

"Elizabeth, shut up," snapped Jacob.

"Girl, why don't you just sit back against the door or something? Leave the card playing to us. It's a man's game, after all," remarked the massive lump of skin as it studied its cards.

"WHAT?" I asked.

"Boy, do you want another card?" asked the thin man.

"Uh, I don't . . ."

"YOU BET WE DO!" I exclaimed.

"ELIZABETH, DON'T!" cried Jacob.

"WE HAVE TO BEAT THEM DON'T WE? OUR CARDS ARE GOOD, BUT WE HAVE TO BE SURE! You don't have to be a man to see that."

The thin man chuckled to himself once again, and as always, the others joined in. Then the bandaged head monster held up one finger, and the thin man threw him a card. The green man did the same. The thin man took no other cards himself, but the blob drew one.

My teeth nibbled at my tongue, trying to punish it for taking another card. But I knew why I did it. Nobody, living or dead like these creatures, could tell Elizabeth Martin that she couldn't play a certain game. If it all ended right here and now, at least I wouldn't give these monsters the satisfaction of knowing I sat back and let it happen.

"We'll keep the anticipation level high on this one," said the thin man. "Schueller, what do you have?"

The bandaged man threw down his cards.

Eighteen.

Then the green man.

Nineteen.

The thin man grinned, then showed us his hand.

Twenty.

The fleshy mass let his cards drop on the floor. The thin man turned them over for him.

Eighteen.

Jacob, sweating a gallon as his adam's apple fixed itself in the middle of his throat, laid down his cards on the floor, for all to see . . .

15

"Twenty-one," said Jacob. "My extra card was a four."

The entire compartment grew very still. No one moved. No one said a word.

Then the thin man broke into laughter. "Boys, I think it's time to find a new trade. We've been beaten by a couple of kids."

"Then we can go?" Jacob asked.

"You can go. Get out of here," said the green man, before placing his face into his hands.

"Wait," I said. "You guys were going to take our money and eat us. Don't we get an added bonus for our win?"

Jacob stared at me coldly. "Uh, Elizabeth. They're letting us walk out of here. That's enough isn't it?"

"No. Please, listen. This train's going to

crash . . ." I started.

"Girlie, we know the train wrecks. We're haunting it aren't we?" the blob spit through his teeth.

"Yes, but we can stop it. We just need to find out who's responsible," I said, suspecting no one in this crowd to be the culprit. They didn't seem the saboteur type to me.

Then, to my shock and horror, the bandaged man removed some of the strips from where his mouth should've been. Something fleshy, like a tongue, rolled out of the opening and dropped on the floor. Flat at first, it quickly inflated itself, revealing an open end which instantly made me think of an elephant's trunk. Then it spoke.

"Talk to Charlie, he's the waiter in the dining car. He serves everybody, he knows everybody," it said with a slurpy voice. Then the creature began tediously rolling his trunk back up with his hands.

"But there is no dining car!" Jacob rang in.

"No dining car?" slobbered the fat one, **"THEN WE BETTER EAT NOW!"**

The monster reached to grab Jacob's leg, but he and I both had moved for the door. On our way out, we saw the fat mass leap into the air, slamming into the door just as we shut it from the other side.

At our wit's end, we made our way to the end of the car, where the tar-covered man leaned against the wall next to the door.

"I see that you got by Headley," he said slyly. "Too bad you had to make friends with those ruffians to do it. They're a nasty bunch."

"What . . . what time is it?" I could hardly catch my breath.

"Why, this watch hasn't worked for a very, very long time. Not since the accident, y'know. Which, by the way, should be coming up here in about forty minutes," the creature said.

"Aw, no," gasped Jacob. "We've . . . we've got to find Charlie, the waiter."

"Oh, you wish to eat, do you? Well, then let's make our way to the dining car, shall we?" the tar-covered man asked, and then opened the car door.

A dining car.

The Fairfield Express didn't have a dining car, yet one lay right before our eyes.

It was completely deserted, and it looked positively revolting.

The walls were moldy, turning green and

brown in large, spoiled areas. Cobwebs floated from the corners, and the mildew in the air could actually be seen. The furniture had mostly rotted, though some pieces had simply been burnt, scorched to a crispy black. And the smell . . . my stomach wanted to curl up and die.

"Just makes you hungry walking in here doesn't it?" the creature asked, then ushered us through the door. He followed us inside and showed us to a booth.

"Where's Charlie?" I asked quickly, wanting to get out of that rat box as soon as possible.

"Doesn't he work here?" asked Jacob.

"Yes, he does. But not too many people ask for him. It can be . . . dangerous." The dead creature sat back, and though his dripping face didn't leave much room for detail, he seemed serious enough. After what I'd been through already, getting myself into more danger felt terribly unnecessary. We'd find an alternative.

"But," said the creature, *if it's Charlie you want it's Charlie you'll get!* **CHARLIE!**"

"**NO!**" I screamed.

16

A roar, so loud and intense it shook the windows, echoed from the next car.

Jacob and I got up to run, but something sticky grabbed my arm. *The tar-covered man!*

"Sit down. It's too late. If he sees you running now, it will only make it worse. By the way, my name's George," he said.

I wanted to punch him, but instead lowered myself back into the seat. "Thanks, George," I growled with clenched teeth.

Jacob saw me staying, and jumped back in the booth. "What is this thing?" he asked. "What's it going to do?"

George leaned in, his chin dripping onto the table. "Just give him your order. Don't stutter, don't stammer, and look him straight in the eyes. Don't try to be friendly, but keep talking for at least a minute. He considers it respectful not to give short orders!"

"What do we order?" I asked, and George handed me a menu from the edge of the table.

I opened it like a present, fast and furious.

"*What is this?* Worm burgers? Mashed bat heads with pond bottom gravy?" My stomach began to churn.

"Yes, it's all good. Now choose your order, I think he's coming," pressed George.

Then something shook the dining car.

As the door to the kitchen car closed, I realized that something had stepped in.

Charlie.

A massive, jaundiced-yellow abomination, towering over everything I'd seen so far. I'll never know how he fit through that door.

Jacob couldn't see him from where he sat, and I don't think he wanted to turn around. However, I'm sure he saw my face, reading every terrible thought that went through my head as the monster came into full view.

I could see his teeth from where he stood, bright red, practically fluorescent. But his eyes looked like eight-balls without the 'eight'; smooth, glossy, and emotionless. Like Jaws, I thought, but no movie monster could ever scare me like this.

At that moment, I was scared to be alive.

Charlie moved forward slowly, knowing we wouldn't go anywhere (my muscles had surrendered and gone to sleep). When he reached the table, my eyes locked onto the veins coursing through his bald head, then to the suit he wore. A fine-fitting waiter's uniform that looked practically new. The nice suit almost made me feel comfortable until . . .

"WHAT IS YOUR ORDER?" he asked, and looked straight at me, teeth glistening in the light.

No air. Suffocating. I couldn't get out any words! But then . . .

"Worm burger, I would like a worm burger. I would like my worms medium-well and on a whole wheat bun if I could. I would also like an order of rat legs, heavily salted, and some catsup to go with that. For a drink, I would like cola with ants in it, and for dessert, I yearn for the roadkill cobbler. But for starters, the cheeks and salsa look good."

There. I'd ordered. I'd looked right into his eyes and ordered, without tripping up once. It didn't quite last a minute, but I couldn't remember any more items from the menu.

In an uneasy silence, Charlie wrote the order on a dingy notepad, then turned to Jacob.

Oh, no.

Jacob's nervous shakes could be seen a mile away. He looked as if he was about to lose it.

Jacob opened his mouth, and . . .

"I, I . . . uh," he stammered.

Charlie stared at him, and we stared at Charlie. Out of the corner of my eye, I saw George sinking in his seat.

Charlie's breathing increased.

His lungs pumped air into his body so heavily, so quickly, he seemed to be growing larger.

He *was* growing larger.

Jacob and I took the signal to move.

I hopped over the back of the booth, just as Charlie roared.

WHAM! *The monster threw his fist all the way through the roof, then pulled it out, only to use it to crush the table where we sat into tiny pieces of wood.*

I climbed over table after table, leaping in the air to grab the handle of the dining car door.

Locked.

What? Why?

Before I could figure it out, Jacob's scream got my attention.

"HELP! HE'S AFTER ME!"

Clambering over some booths and scrambling under others, Jacob fled for his life, as Charlie ripped into seats and tables trying to grab him.

The chase led in my direction.

Shoving my foot against a booth for support, I pulled at the handle until it hurt. The door wouldn't budge.

As I scanned the floor, searching desperately for something to use to break the window, my time ran out.

Jacob leaped from the last booth and came crashing down on top of me. Like a bulldozer, Charlie followed. And he followed fast.

Too fast to stop himself.

His head plowed right into the door, crashing through the glass and pushing the walls around the frame outward to touch the next car.

We jumped to our feet, bulleting down the aisle to the next door.

When I grabbed the handle . . .

Locked again.

"NO!" I screamed.

Charlie pulled free from the wall. Turning to us, he stalked slowly down the aisle.

His prey was trapped . . .

17

Charlie's eyes developed tiny, red pupils as he came closer, his clawed hands outstretched, ready to crush one of us in each of them.

Jacob slammed against the door, beating himself up trying to get out. He even rammed his fist into the glass, but it didn't crack at all. Too thick. I know because I beat on it, too. Jacob and I pounded that door with everything we had, crying and screaming and begging, until Charlie's hulking shadow fell over us.

Then someone appeared at the door.

A girl. A beautiful, young girl, surrounded by a brilliant, golden aura that brightened the dining car even through the glass.

"Charlie," she said. "I want some water."

Her words seemed to sing in my head, and I had to tear my eyes away from her to see Charlie.

He'd stopped.

His anger seemed to be dying. He lowered his arms, and the red in his eyes again turned to a glossy black, but reflected the golden light from the window. With every beat of my heart, he came down in size, until pretty soon he returned to his former height, if not smaller.

Then he reached out between Jacob and me, and pulled the door open, popping the lock off into the air.

"I tried to get some from the kitchen, but everyone was busy," she said in a soothing tone.

"I'll get it for you," Charlie said, and made his way into the next car.

I stood there, letting my adrenalin drain, telling my heart to come back to normal, and asking myself if it had all just happened.

Jacob had fallen against the wall, his face damp with sweat. The veins in his forehead visibly throbbed. I peeled him off the paneling and we followed Charlie and the girl into the next car.

Charlie walked behind the counter, growled at the cook (a short man with no bottom jaw), then grabbed a pitcher and poured a nice, cool glass of water. No dirt, no bugs, just water.

Then he handed it over the counter to the girl.

"Thank you, Charlie," she said, and patted his hand.

"He's become a big teddy bear," I whispered to Jacob as we moved further in.

"What do we do now? This didn't get us anywhere," Jacob pointed out.

"Let's follow her," I said. "No one seems to be giving her trouble. Plus, she's the most normal looking one of the bunch."

"I'll say. Hubba, hubba," Jacob whispered.

"What?" I shot back.

"She's probably the prettiest girl I've ever seen, er, besides you, of course. But *she* can't beat me up!" he explained.

"You don't know that," I told him.

"Sure I do. Look at her. She's ill. She's probably not even supposed to be up!" he said.

"She's dead, Jacob, that's as ill as it gets. Now come on!" I moved forward, nervously passing Charlie, who still stood behind the counter as the girl walked away.

Halfway there . . .

"GOOD NIGHT!" he screamed, sending

Jacob and I running up the hall, almost crashing into the girl we followed.

Once we saw that Charlie wasn't chasing us, we held back, watching the girl glide through the next dining car like a true spirit. Even the dead stopped eating to take in her sight. I barely noticed my awful surroundings, keeping my eye on the girl with the feeling she'd lead us out of here herself.

She went through the next door, and as we followed behind her, *I felt a hand grip my shoulder, and another grab my arm.*

"I wouldn't follow her if I were you," the voice from behind said.

George.

I spun around, pulling my arms from his gooey, sopping grasp.

"You! How'd you get away from Charlie?" I asked, a little louder and much bolder than I may have intended.

He stepped back, surprised by my daring tone. He explained, "I can be pretty slippery when I want to be."

"Come on, Elizabeth, let's go!" Jacob pulled me by the arm, and began to follow when George held me back again.

"Let go of me!" I warned.

The passengers around me started getting upset, and for the first time since I entered the car I took a good look at them. Hideous ghouls, piled and packed on top of each other like luggage, squirmed in their seats. Those that had eyes beamed at me with nervous, uneasy expressions on their faces.

I could feel their tension.

"That girl is Carla Ledger. The Mayor's daughter," said George. "Why are you following her?"

I felt the restlessness around me. A couple of the passengers stood up, waiting on my answer.

At the time, I didn't know why we followed her, but my brain kicked in an answer. "We're following her so she can lead us to the Mayor."

For some reason, that made George all the more suspicious, because then he asked, "Why do you want to see the Mayor?"

More of the dead stood up, waiting on my answer.

Jacob gave it for me. "Because we have personal business, that's why," he said.

Everything grew silent.

Then George turned around, facing the crowd of ghastly passengers whose raspy breaths suddenly became more audible.

"I'm an acquaintance of the Mayor's," he said. "I know that in the past few weeks he's gotten a few letters. Threatening letters, from someone who wants to do him in. I also have an acquaintance named Schueller, who's seated up at the front of the train. You two met him. He says you were asking questions. Questions about sabotaging this train . . ." He spun around, his eyes locked on us and his finger pointing accusingly. "Who asks questions about sabotage, *unless they're saboteurs?*"

What?

No, he couldn't be doing this . . .

The monsters began to move.

"YOU CAN'T BE SERIOUS," I yelled over the building growls. "WE'RE KIDS! WHAT DO WE KNOW ABOUT SABOTAGING A TRAIN?!"

"WE'VE BEEN MAKING THIS TRIP FOR OVER A HUNDRED YEARS!" said George. "IT'S THE FIRST TIME WE'VE HEARD OF SABOTAGE, AND IT'S THE FIRST TIME WE'VE SEEN YOU!"

"RUN, ELIZABETH!" yelled Jacob, as he tore down the aisle.

The dead monsters climbed over themselves on their way out of their seats, and I didn't wait a second more. I streaked after Jacob as the dead reached out after me from both sides, grabbing my shirt, pulling my hair, and scratching my skin. One of them latched onto my ankle, and I tripped . . .

19

Hitting the floor, I felt their hands grip my legs. Moist and abrasive, like wet beach sand, and painful, too.

"NOOOOOO!" I flipped over and kicked at them, knocking off pieces of fingers, breaking off legs. I twisted back around, and my fingers tore into the carpet as I pulled myself across the floor. "JACOB, HELP!" A weight came down on top of me, pinning me to the floor. Then two hands wrapped around my head, and started to pull. "JACOB!"

I heard someone yell, and saw a flash of Jacob's body flying over me. He hit something, and my body lurched back further, bending my spine to its breaking point. Then the grip on my head loosened, the weight on my back fell off. I took my chance to run.

Spindly arms reached out for me as I ran to the door, but I knocked them away, grabbed the door latch and flung it open.

Jacob.

As the ghouls moved in on me, I could barely make him out. He fought for freedom from the center of an encircling ghastly mass. The creatures piled on top of him as he frantically punched and kicked.

"JACOB! NO, JACOB!"

The monsters were at the door.

To even have a chance, I'd have to close it shut . . .

"WAIT!"

Jacob burst from the bottom of them, and speared through the doorway just as I slammed the passage shut.

"JACOB! FIND A LOCK! FIND SOMETHING!" I yelled, trying to keep the opening sealed from the ghouls pulling from the other side.

Jacob's luck still held. He found a chain and padlock just beside the door. He weaved it through the latch as I held it, then clamped the lock shut.

We both jumped away, watching the monsters

bash themselves into the door.

"It'll only take them a few minutes to get through," I said, turning around to find . . .

Another carload of passengers, looking extremely uneasy, a few already beginning to get up.

"Let's walk quickly. Let's not say a word," I whispered, and Jacob followed me down the aisle.

The ghouls stood up as we passed them, but not one made a move toward us. They didn't know what had gone on in the last car, and wouldn't until that door gave way, which I hoped wouldn't be too soon.

Then at the end of the hall, the worst of all things stepped from behind a curtain.

Mumfrey, carrying Headley the ticketmaster.

"Oh, no," Jacob whispered.

"Shhh . . ." I said.

I thought we could just walk past them. I hoped there would be no reason to check our tickets since the train left so long ago. I prayed he wouldn't stop us.

As we reached the door, Mumfrey blocked our way. His gaunt face stared down at us, emotionless, uncaring.

Then he held up Headley's head.

"Where do you to think you're going?" he asked.

Think, Elizabeth. Think.

20

"Our mom is sitting back there," I said quickly, trying to make the most of my age.

Headley's head grimaced. "I don't think so. This next car is empty for security reasons."

If he noticed the hammering mob at the other end of the car, it'd all be over.

"But I'm sure she went back here," I insisted. "Can't we go back and check?"

"The Mayor has cleared this car to make sure his daughter stays safe," Headley explained, looking us up and down.

Behind him, I could see two guards posted at the far door of the next car. The door between them opened, and a short, pudgy ghoul, with blue skin and abnormally huge bumps all over its body, stepped out and started yelling up at them.

That had to be the Mayor.

If we could get to him and warn him, maybe he could stop this whole disaster.

Then Mumfrey's head lifted, and gazed down at the opposite door.

He lifted Headley to see, and I heard the window crash in.

"SABOTEURS!" yelled the monstrous herd as they poured through the passenger car doors. "STOP THE SABOTEURS!"

Headley's eyes locked on us.

"WHERE ARE YOUR TICKETS?!" he asked.

I didn't think.

I moved.

My hands grabbed Headley's ears, yanked him away from Mumfrey's grasp, and launched him down the aisle where he landed in the middle of the oncoming mob.

Mumfrey let out an agonized cry, and ran for his partner, stampeding over all who got in his way. He tore through the crowd, desperately searching for Headley.

"COME ON! THROUGH THE DOOR!" Jacob yelled, sliding through the opening to the next car.

Jumping to the other car, I found him pulling another chain from the floor, and he quickly spooled it through the latch and locked it.

"WHAT ARE YOU DOING?" called a voice behind us.

The Mayor stood with his guards, two stocky, pink-scaled, snake-eyed creatures that instantly moved toward us.

"Jacob . . . trouble," I said softly, hoping my friend wouldn't freak.

"What now?" he asked, whirling around.

They inched toward us like snakes about to strike a couple of white mice. Jacob and I shuffled about, looking for a hole to run through. But they'd catch us. I knew they would.

"WE WANT TO HELP YOU," I said. "THERE'S A SABOTEUR ON THIS TRAIN! WE'RE TRYING TO FIND HIM AND STOP HIM!"

The Mayor eyed us for a long moment. Between the thundering army of monsters trapped behind us and the slithering duo creeping ever-so-much-closer, my blood began to dry up, waiting on the Mayor's next move.

"WHO TOLD YOU TWO THERE WAS A

SABOTEUR?" asked the Mayor.

"ODD JOHN," I answered. "HE SAYS HE DIDN'T WRECK THE TRAIN. HE LOVES IT TOO MUCH!"

Mayor Ledger considered my response for a moment, then signaled his troops to halt.

"Of course Odd John didn't wreck the train. Do you think I'd let a maniac run the train my daughter was on? I've always suspected a saboteur myself, but we're powerless to do anything about it."

The fists hammered the door behind us. Again, I heard the glass shatter and hit the floor.

"THE REST OF THE PASSENGERS THINK WE'RE THE SABOTEURS!" Jacob yelled. "CAN YOU HELP US?"

"GUARDS!" yelled the Mayor. "CONTAIN THE MOB!"

The two creatures shot by us with amazing speed, and braced themselves against the door. Producing wooden batons from their holsters, they beat the crowd back through the window, all except one.

A black mass jumped through the window, making a sound like a drain unclogging. The lump rolled on the floor, then jumped to his feet.

George.

"MAYOR," he said, "THERE'S SOME-THING YOU HAVE TO KNOW!"

"DON'T BELIEVE HIM MAYOR!" I screamed. "WE'RE NOT SABOTEURS!"

"I believe you, kids," the Mayor reassured us, then turned his attention to George, ready to get to the bottom of things. "Sir, you're mistak-en."

"Oh I know these kids aren't the saboteurs. They couldn't be," George said slyly, then opened his vest and revealed his terrible secret.

The vest was lined with multiple sticks of DYNAMITE.

"THEY'RE NOT YOUR SABOTEURS," he yelled. "**I AM**."

21

Everyone in the car froze.

Then the guards started moving in, only to stop when George struck a match, and held it right over one of the fuses.

"I think you want to stay back," he warned them.

"Who are you?" asked the Mayor.

George turned to him, a small creak coming from his lowering jaw. His feet pulled from the floor like velcro, as he strode closer to the Mayor, like a curious cat.

"Mayor, Mayor, Mayor. I may not have the looks I once did, but surely you haven't forgotten your former business partner?" George teased him with just enough information.

"George Finley?" the Mayor gasped.

George Who? I thought. *I'd never heard of*

this guy!

"We could've made it rich in the big city, Donald!" George Finley cried. "But you, you wanted to become the Mayor of Fairfield, and took your half of the business with you! I lost everything after that, Donald! Everything! Well, now you're going to pay! I'll blow you up, along with this miserable, little train that serves your miserable, little town!"

A business venture. The train wreck had nothing to do with the train, the railroad, or Odd John at all.

"And to think these brats almost stopped me from destroying it all again," he continued.

"**YOU RAT!**" Jacob screamed. "You kept putting us in danger! You tried to get us out of the way so you'd be clear to blow up the train!"

"What amazing brains the living have," George said, lowering the match to the fuse. "But I think it's high time we end this little stand-off **with a big bang!**"

"GEORGE, WAIT!" yelled the Mayor, getting George's attention as he pulled the brake cord.

Why didn't we think of that?

But nothing happened.

"YOU FIEND!" the Mayor cursed. "You

thought of everything, didn't you?"

To our surprise, George looked a little stunned.

"I . . . I didn't cut the brake cord," he said, just as the door behind the Mayor opened and the room filled with light.

The Mayor's daughter emerged from the room, glowing even brighter than before, but looking very sickly.

"Father, what is happening?" she asked, filling the room with a beautiful harmony.

"CARLA, GET BACK!" the Mayor yelled.

But George took his chance.

He lit one of the dynamite sticks, and flung it into Carla's room.

"NO!" I yelled.

Maniacally cackling, he lit the rest of sticks, then tossed them throughout the car.

Before we could react, the door behind the guards burst open . . .

And in flooded the dead.

A ghastly, ghostly riot.

22

"CARLA!" The Mayor cried, diving into the other car to retrieve the deadly explosive George had sent that way.

My eyes bounced back and forth from the oncoming wall of hideousness the passengers formed, to the sparkling stick of red death that rolled across the floor, coming closer to me.

"THE WINDOW! BREAK A WINDOW!" I shrieked at the Mayor's guards, and they instantly caught on. One of them crashed his club into the glass, shattering it into a million pieces.

My mind screamed at me not to try what my pitching arm knew I could do. In one motion, I scooped up a stick of dynamite, and pitched it at the open window. I didn't breathe until it went through.

Jacob grabbed another one, and fired it at the window.

It bounced off the side and came my way. A grounder. Snatching it from the floor, I shot it past the watching heads of the dead, to join its companion out the window.

"GIRLIE!" screamed one of the ghouls. "HERE'S ANOTHER!" He tossed me what had to be shortest lit fuse I'd seen yet, but I matched my first two pitches, sending it hurtling outside the train.

"ANY MORE?!" I yelled, then I heard a scream.

Inside Carla's car, Mayor Ledger and George Finley were engaged in a struggle over the last burning explosive.

"THERE'S YOUR SABOTEUR!" I announced, just as the two came smashing through the doorway and onto the floor, tearing at each other like animals.

But George had control of the dynamite.

He lobbed it over Mayor Ledger's head, and back into Carla's car.

Before I could move, Jacob darted past me. Leaping over the two fighters, he landed in Carla's car, and grabbed the dynamite.

"HER'S IS THE LAST CAR, SON! THROW IT OUT THE BACK!" The Mayor screamed.

I had to help him. Racing down the aisle, I hopped over George and the Mayor, blew past Carla, and had almost caught up with Jacob when he reached the door. Stopping beside him, I ripped the door open, and Jacob launched the explosive out the back.

Not five seconds later, we felt the thunderous blast destroy the track behind us.

Shaking, we both fell to the floor, unable to say a word.

Through my daze, I saw Mayor Ledger making his way down the aisle, dragging George Finley behind him. He stopped a few yards short of us.

"Thank you," he said. "You've saved us all." Then he turned to the misshapen crowd behind him. "This man's crime deserves a serious punishment. That punishment . . . is your revenge. He's yours, folks." And with that, the Mayor dropped George in a heap on the floor, and the crowd moved in on him.

Then, at once, they pounced.

Jacob and I watched the gruesome scene for a few moments, and then when George's screaming finally died off, Jacob had a question for me.

"Why isn't this over, yet? We found the saboteur. Why aren't we stopping?"

"The Mayor said the brake lines had been cut," I said.

"Yeah, but George said he didn't do it," remarked Jason.

That's when the gunshot went off.

The ghouls cleared the aisle, and at the end of it, stood four familiar figures.

Our card buddies. The thin man. The filthy blob. The green man. And Schueller.

"I'm sorry for the noise," said the thin man, lowering his smoking gun after firing it into the ceiling. "But we're here on behalf of Odd John Cape. You see, he's got a little business left with this train, and he's paid us good money to see that no one interferes. Namely, those two," he said, and pointed straight at Jacob and me.

We'd been double-crossed . . .

23

"Sutter's Pass should be coming up any time now," the thin man continued. "That's where he's going to do it. Then all of this will be over."

Every nerve in my body collapsed as I slid to the floor.

We failed. Nothing we had done mattered at all. The train would still crash, but this time Jacob and I would be on it.

"I can't believe this," I muttered, dropping my head against my knees.

Then Jacob drew close to me and whispered, "We're not done yet."

What?

"After all, this is the last car. I saw a ladder going to the roof," he said softly.

"You're crazy," I said. *The roof? Way too dangerous.*

"Desperate times call for desperate measures," he answered. "We just need a diversion, and I think I've got an idea."

Jacob stood, his legs wobbling just a little.

The thin man tensed, as did his cohorts, ready to act at the slightest sign of escape.

"If it's all going to be over very shortly," he began, "then I'd like to do something I might not get the chance to later. I'd like to speak with Carla. I'd like to ask her a question."

A question?

For the life of me I couldn't figure him out. Where could he be going with this?

Obviously, the thin man knew.

A smile crossed his face, and soon that signature chuckle of his broke the silence. As to be expected, the whole gang joined in on his laughter.

"Okay," the thin man said. "If you want to make friends, you've got a few minutes left. Go ahead."

Jacob walked up to the center of the car where Carla sat, and stood facing her.

"I just wanted to ask you," said Jacob, "where can I get a glass of water around here?"

For the first time, I saw Carla smile.

Then, with lungs I never would have guessed she had, Carla screamed, **"CHARLIE! HELP!"**

The thin man grabbed her instantly, and the green man held back the Mayor as Jacob galloped back toward me.

In the distance, three cars down, I saw him coming down the aisle.

Charlie.

Tables, luggage, and even seats were torn out of his way as he stormed through each car, coming closer.

The gambling quartet panicked, hiding themselves behind the other passengers and crawling under seats.

I even think I heard them scream as Charlie ripped through the doors, instantly grabbing the blob, who couldn't move fast at all, and smashed him against the wall like a rotten tomato.

"LET'S MOVE!" Jacob yelled, pulling the door open.

As I got to my feet, the inhuman shrieks of the thin man filled the air as Charlie pulled him like a giant rubber band.

The entire crowd tried to take cover, but the battle raged out of control.

I saw Mayor Ledger grab Carla and hop into a corner, out of the way.

Jacob grabbed me and pulled me through the door just as Schueller jumped for us. He didn't make it. Jacob slammed it quickly, right on Schueller's head. It exploded in a puff of hair, and his trunk shot straight out to hang off the end of the car.

"**THERE**," Jacob pointed to the ladder right off the car's back step. "**AFTER YOU.**"

Not only did I have second thoughts, I had thirds and fourths.

But we were running out of time.

I stepped up onto the ladder and started climbing to the top. The cold air swept over me, feeling like a new skin. And the higher I went, the worse it got. When I reached the top, I saw what rigors lay ahead.

We'd been through eight cars, and now we'd have to cross them again, the hard way.

Feeling Jacob pushing me, I climbed up and stepped onto the roof.

The force of the air practically sent me sailing. Crouching down, I used my hands to guide me along. I realized that if we went from car to car at that speed, we'd never make it in time.

Jacob crawled up beside me.

"I THINK WE'RE GOING TO HAVE TO MAKE A DASH FOR IT," I yelled over the wind.

"WE'LL HAVE TO! THERE'S SUTTER'S PASS!" he shouted, pointing to an opening between two large hills, maybe five miles up the track.

Then let's do it, I thought, raising up slightly, and moving forward.

We stayed one behind the other, me in front. My footing felt unsure on the first couple of cars, but by the end of third, I started feeling more confident. Jacob must've felt a little cocky, too. He came up beside me, almost like we were racing. We jumped to the fourth car, then the fifth, and then the sixth. By the seventh we felt like pros, our biggest mistake.

Jacob took a long jump, and his feet came out from under him.

He slid over the side.

I screamed out to him, and my heart returned to my chest when I saw his hand clinging to the roof railing.

I let myself slip down, bringing my foot to rest right beside his hand.

When I looked over the edge at him, I saw him looking ahead of the train and not up at me.

Then his head snapped up, his eyes met mine, filled with terror.

"PULL ME UP, ELIZABETH! PULL ME UP!"

I looked ahead of the train.

A tree. Growing right next to the track.

It'd shave Jacob off like a bad whisker.

25

My hands wrapped around his arm and pulled, yanking Jacob up enough for him to get his foot on the railing.

His sense of self-preservation did the rest.

He launched himself up onto the roof once again as the tree passed by, slapping and scraping the train with its outstretched limbs.

We didn't waste any time patting ourselves on the back. Hopping back up, we jumped to car number eight, and at its end, took a careful look down at what awaited us.

The steam engine.

Once again, my eyes became blinded by the clouds of steam that pumped from the top of the engine. I strained to see even a silouhette of the mad engineer, Odd John Cape.

"Where is he?" Jacob whispered.

"We won't know unless we get down there," I said. "Maybe we can at least make it to the engine and try to stop the train."

"I don't see a ladder here," Jacob said. "We'll have to jump."

"After you," I remarked.

Jacob took a deep breath, stood up, and jumped, landing with a loud clang on the tender car below.

Then I stood and got ready to jump, just as a cloud of steam swept over the tender, completely hiding Jacob. When it cleared, Jacob had disappeared.

26

My throat swelled as my heart filled it. Looking down, I didn't see any sign of Jacob, and no indication of Odd John, either.

I'd have to go down there.

Rising, I steadied myself right at the edge of the car, and leaped. Slamming hard on the tender car's floor, the steam seemed to almost attack me, filling my lungs and eyes with its heavy smoke.

"JACOB!" I yelled. "WHERE ARE YOU?"

Nothing.

I got to my feet, moving slowly around the clouded car, circling the tender.

Just as I turned the corner, I saw Jacob moving carefully toward the deserted engine.

THEN FROM BEHIND HIM, SPRANG ODD JOHN!

He had his coal shovel pulled back, ready to smash Jacob in the head!

"JACOB, DUCK!" I shrieked.

He hit the floor, just as Odd John brought the shovel around.

"I WILL NOT BE DENIED MY DEATH!" Odd John screamed, once again lifting the shovel above his head, ready to bring it down on Jacob.

Instinctively, I rushed, giving the ghoulish engineer a mid-body tackle. He grunted, stopping his attack. But it didn't knock him over.

It made him mad.

With his filthy claw, he grabbed the back of my shirt and lifted me high into the air.

"NO, DON'T!" I yelled, begging him not to . . . *throw me.*

It felt like being on some kind of ride, because it seemed so effortless for him to pick me up and launch me across the front of the tender *and almost off the train.*

Reaching my hands out for the closest thing to grab, I managed to snag the iron ladder attached to the corner of the steam engine. I felt the toe of my foot barely nick the spinning wheels below me, giving me all the incentive I needed to lift my legs and pull my feet back up onto the platform.

Jacob growled, locking himself onto Odd John's legs, trying to pull him off his feet.

Trying to pull him off his feet. It reminded me of Jacob's idea to push Odd John off the train when we first met him! If we could get Odd John off the train, the haunting would end, and the ghost train would cease to run.

"**ELIZABETH!**" Jacob screamed.

Odd John had gotten hold of him, wrapped his hands around his neck and started choking him.

"For over a hundred years," Odd John said, "I've never been able to carry out my wishes! My train was sabotaged, blown up before I could wreck her myself, stealing from us the perfect burial that this beautiful engine and I deserved! But I'm going to bury us this time! I'm going to bury us all!"

Looking into the engine, I saw a wrench braced against the throttle. If I pulled it out, the train would slow down. And if I laid on the brakes, I could probably stop the engine before we hit Sutter's Pass.

Jacob was gasping for air, kicking and

punching at John to let him go, but the dead engineer kept adding pressure, squeezing the life out of my friend.

I had to save him, but I was so close to stopping the train . . .

27

"**LET HIM GO!**" I yelled, running over to the battling duo, and picking up John's shovel from the floor.

Odd John looked down at me just as I slammed the spade into his legs, breaking them apart at the knees.

The ghost screamed like he felt it, dropping Jacob and falling to the floor. I spun around to climb back to the engine and remove the wrench, but Odd John's bony fingers dug into my ankle, holding me back from going anywhere.

Wincing in pain, I screamed to Jacob, "PULL THE WRENCH FROM THE THROTTLE. THEN SLAM ON THE BRAKE!" His blue face slowly began turning flesh colored again, his eyes shrinking back to normal. I could tell he had no idea what I was talking about.

"YOU'RE NOT GOING TO END THIS FOR ME, DO YOU HEAR? IF I'M NOT DRIVING THIS ENGINE, NO ONE WILL BE!" screamed Odd John, reaching between the engine and the tender car.

Then he pulled something up in his hand.

The carriage key.

The very thing that held the two cars together.

In panic, I grabbed hold of the ladder at the center of the engine's back floor.

Odd John rolled back with the tender car, but still had a death-grip on my ankle.

"JACOB!" I screamed.

He came bouncing out of the engineer's cab, with the wrench in his hand.

I instantly noticed the engine slowing, and the tender car began to close back in on the engine.

"PUT IT BACK!" I screamed. "THEN COME BACK AND HELP ME!"

I had to take that chance to end Odd John's terror. If we could get him far enough from the engine, I hoped his spirit would no longer control the train.

With a slight jerk, the train's speed began to increase.

I felt my hands slipping from the ladder. Odd John pulled my leg harder, trying to yank me straight from the train and onto the tracks below.

Not far off from happening.

My left hand slipped, leaving my good hand, my pitching hand, to bear the burden of holding me there, anchoring my human bridge.

Finally, Jacob locked his grip around my left hand.

"**PULL!**" The command burst from my lips.

Jacob gritted his teeth, tugging my arm until I felt sure it sprang loose from its socket.

I caught a glimpse of the tender car, slowing down behind us, and I felt Odd John's arms lock.

"**NOOOOOooooo!**" he screamed.

But, I still felt his hands on my legs.

Jacob pulled me up to the floor, and I quickly looked down at my ankles, *WHERE ODD JOHN STILL CLUNG DESPERATELY TO ME.*

"IT'S MY TRAIN! IT'S MY TRAIN!" he cried in begging agony. "WE BELONG TOGETHER!"

Then, piece by piece, the track began to knock him apart.

First, the rest of his legs broke off and bounced down the rails, making him lose his grip slightly.

Then his ribs hit the track, and it was all over for him. From there, the boards tore him to bits instantly, leaving only his hands, arms, collar bone, and head.

SUDDENLY HE PULLED HIMSELF UP, ATTEMPTING TO TAKE A BITE RIGHT OUT OF MY FACE!

But I punched him, and as he went down, I grabbed his engineer cap. Odd John's skull hit the track, taking the rest of him with it.

It bounced a few times, and then rolled to a stop.

"HE'S GONE," Jacob yelled, "BUT THE TRAIN'S NOT SLOWING DOWN!"

We shot up, and climbed into the engineer's cab. To our horror, we'd run out of time.

The train turned into the terrible curve known as Sutter's Pass.

Jacob pulled the wrench from the throttle.

I slammed on the brake.

We both closed our eyes, and prayed for a miracle.

28

The train came to a sudden, complete stop.

We both screamed, then fell silent. My insides wanted to leap out. Our bodies jerked forward, but it was only reactionary.

I was afraid to open my eyes.

"WE'RE PARKED!" Jacob yelled, falling back into the instrument panel in heaving relief.

We stood in the Fairfield Express' engine, parked in the same spot it had been when we found it, back at the Fairfield Train Depot.

"We must've finally ended the haunting!" I reasoned.

"But how'd we get back here? Jacob asked.

"I have no idea. Maybe we never left it to begin with. The whole thing might have been some kind of delusion. It could have all occurred in our heads," I said, seeing an expression of total disagreement building on Jacob's face.

"Or maybe we were on some other plane of existence. Maybe the ghosts pulled us into their world!" he exclaimed.

"I don't know. I just want to get out of here before it happens again!" I said, pulling myself from against the instruments and moving to the back of the engine.

Just as we stepped out, we were engulfed in a bright, blinding light.

29

"WHAT ARE YOU KIDS DOING HERE?" a voice asked.

Ivan.

Ivan Brewer. Everyone knew him as the scariest security guard around. *Mr. Davenport did hire him to watch the train.*

He kept his flashlight on us until he got close, and felt sure we couldn't get away.

"I want answers," he said, standing before us like a super-soldier interrogating prisoners of war.

"We just wanted to see the train," I said. "We didn't touch anything."

"We've never seen a real steam engine before," Jacob added. "You know, they don't make them anymore."

Ivan eyed us as if we were a couple of

lowly criminals.

"There have been some snoopers around this train all week. That's why Mr. Davenport hired me. Looks like you're my suspects," Ivan said.

No way. I hadn't been through that whole adventure just to get blamed for something I didn't do.

"Sir, please," I said softly. "This train . . . it's haunted."

"*Haunted?*" he asked. He looked shocked.

"Well, it *was* haunted," Jacob rang in. "But we just solved that problem!"

Ivan appeared nervous. He obviously didn't like the idea of a haunted train. He even backed up a couple of steps.

"You kids go on," he said, staring at the steam engine. "Get home."

Unreal. I stood stunned for a second, but then felt Jacob's hand grab my arm and begin to pull me away. Then I noticed Ivan's wristwatch.

"Could you tell me what time it is?" I asked.

"Ten 'til seven," said Ivan. "Now go, both of you!"

I didn't need Jacob to pull me. We both ran off. I only turned my head once to see Ivan carefully climbing on-board the engine, shining his light over every inch. I'd heard rumors that Ivan believed in the supernatural, which would explain why the ghost train made him feel uneasy. But he still felt the need to search it.

Well, he could scour every inch of that engine. I'd never set foot on-board it again.

"Did you hear what time it was?" I said to Jacob as we climbed the hill out of the depot.

"What?" Jacob asked.

"Ten 'til seven," I told him. "We've got ten minutes to make it to the theater and meet my mom!"

30

It took us six minutes at top speed. No problem for me, but Jacob practically passed out. Only the prospect of my mom, catching us running up to the theater when we should've been inside to begin with, powered us along like rockets. When we got to the Gideon 8, Mom's car pulled in at the far corner of the parking lot.

We had a few precious seconds to catch our breaths. Sneaking into the restrooms inside, we wiped our faces free of sweat, and I grabbed a much-needed handful of water to slurp.

Exiting at the same time, we made our way down the red, entrance ramp and back outside.

Mom honked at us instantly.

We made our way to the car and hopped in. *Ahhh, she had the air conditioner on.*

"Hey, Mom, what's up?" I greeted her.

She stared at me for a second, then turned to Jacob, looking him over just as closely.

"What? What is it?" I asked.

"Both of you look so pale," she said. "That must've been some movie."

Telling her about our adventure meant telling her we never stayed at the theater to see the movie.

"So tell me about the picture," Mom said. "Was it worth the wait?"

Ohh . . . the guilt. I'd end up telling her. I knew it. I never could keep secrets from her. I gave Jacob a look, showing him my surrendering expression, and he frowned and nodded.

"Well, you see Mom, it all started with these two kids sneaking onto a train . . . "

About the Authors

Marty M. Engle and **Johnny Ray Barnes Jr.**, graduates of the Art Institute of Atlanta, are the creators, writers, designers and illustrators of the **Strange Matter™ series and the Strange Matter™ World Wide Web page.**

Their interests and expertise range from state of the art 3-D computer graphics and interactive multi-media, to books and scripts (television and motion picture).

Marty lives in La Jolla, California with his wife Jana and twin terror pets, Polly and Oreo.

Johnny Ray lives in Tierrasanta, California and spends every free moment with his fiancée, Meredith.

And now
an exciting preview
of the next

#13 Toy Trouble
by Marty M. Engle

1

"Clear the way! Clear the way! Car crash victim coming through!" I yelled through the paper dust-mask fixed tightly over my nose and mouth. "A beautiful young woman's life is in our hands!" Already I could feel the adrenalin rushing through me, the familiar pounding in my chest.

I pushed her along the carpet, toward the awaiting operating area.

"Pupils fixed and dilated," I muttered, staring down at the victim's perfect face. Her blue eyes stared up at me, unblinking. I could feel them staring into me, trusting me with her very life. I would not fail her. I *could* not fail her, as I had failed the others.

I'm Karen Sanders, 11 years old. As chief surgeon of the ER, I see a lot of **tragic cases** pass through these doors, but this had to be one of the worst.

"What's the story on this one?" Nurse Fuzzy Bear asked, moving swiftly to the operating table.

"Slammed by a pink convertible in front of her dream house. Get me a crash cart and one of those electro-cardio thingies with all the monitors and dials! NOW!"

Instantly, Nurse Fuzzy Bear and her friends shoved the hi-tech medical equipment to the operating table.

"HEY!" I yelled, catching Blueberry Muffin's™ attention. "Do you consider a berry-scented dress with a big, floppy hat a standard nurse's uniform?"

She hung her large head in shame.

"No time for you to change into something more appropriate! Get the electro-paddle shockers. NOW!" I demanded.

Big Jake™ moved silently up beside me, ready to move the victim from the roller-cart thing to the operating table. His bare, muscular arms reached down and . . .

"DON'T MOVE HER HEAD!" I cried, warning him. "She may have a fractured neck or something! ON THREE! One . . . two . . . three . . . GO!"

Big Jake™, Nurse Fuzzy Bear and I

moved the poor woman to the operating table. Her whole body seemed stiff as a board. Her long, blond hair seemed unnaturally wiry.

Wasting no time, I pulled the desk lamp over her face. My top-flight surgical team went to work.

"Plastic tubing. NOW!" I yelled.

Nurse Fuzzy Bear finished taping the tubes to both of the victims' arms. "Arms and legs stiff and skinny! No noticeable joints!"

"Just as I suspected," I mumbled, pushing my finger against her head, feeling it wobble back and forth. "The free-rolling ball joint is coming loose." My heart sank. I'd seen this before.

"FLATLINE!" Nurse Blueberry Muffin™ called from the electro-cart thing.

"CLEAR!" I yelled.

Instantly, my crew fell away from the operating table as I plunged the foam paddles with their curly cords down onto the victim's chest, hoping the shock would bring her back.

I pressed my ear down to her chest. *Nothing.*

"CLEAR!" I yelled again.

The crew glanced nervously at each other.

They knew I wouldn't give up, not even when it was too late. They didn't say a word, just stared at each other with glassy eyes.

I pressed my ear down to her chest.

Nothing.

"C'mon! Don't give up on me now! You have too much to live for! Think of your vast wardrobe, your dream house, your long, stylable hair! FIGHT! FIGHT!" I cried, plunging the foam paddles down onto her again.

"WE HAVE A HEARTBEAT! You did it, Dr. Sanders," Blueberry Muffin™ gasped, never taking her eyes from her monitor.

The crew breathed a sigh of relief.

Then the victim's head fell off!

"NO!" I gasped. "QUICK! NURSE FUZZY BEAR! STICK THAT BACK ON!"

The crew panicked, scrambling for even more expensive equipment.

"The head's no good," Nurse Fuzzy Bear cried, inspecting the hollow interior.

"Big Jake™! Replacement head! Hurry! We're losing time!" I yelled.

Quickly, he and I rummaged through the shoebox full of replacement heads. Mostly blondes. A redhead. Nothing quite . . . Hmmm.

Decisions like these are why I'm the head

surgeon. The incredible pressure and mind-numbing stress have destroyed lesser surgeons, but not I, Karen Sanders, M.D.

I made my decision.

"Hollow or not, that head's going back on! Super-glue. NOW!" I cried as gasps and applause erupted from the crew.

I popped the top off the tube of Super-glue and squeezed out just a drop onto the rounded stump of the neck.

"Such finesse," Nurse Fuzzy Bear remarked.

"That's why I'm head honcho," I muttered, finishing the job. The head fit back on perfectly . . . *but would it stay?* I winced as I remembered the ones that hadn't.

"Keep an eye on her vitals," I said, pulling my mask off, sighing and rubbing my forehead. "I'll tell ya' Nurse Fuzzy Bear. This is the part I hate . . . talking to the boyfriend."

With head bowed, I approached the boyfriend, seated stiffly on the floor. *What a brave man,* I thought to myself. Despite the incredible strain he must be feeling, his hair was perfect and his mouth was fixed in a wide smile.

"The truth, doctor. Please. Will she make

it?" he asked, disguising the fear that must have been tearing him apart inside.

I looked sheepishly down and said quietly, "One moment . . ."

I quickly grabbed my eight ball and started shaking it, thinking to myself, "Will SunFun Darcy™ live?"

I turned the eight ball over and gazed down at the little round window, licking my lips, anxiously awaiting the answer.

Tragedy or triumph?

The little triangle came into view, fuzzy in the blue liquid, bouncing slightly. . . then the answer . . . **Ask again later.**

I mumbled to myself, shrugging. "That's the way the ol' eight ball bounces."

With every ounce of strength and poise I could muster, I turned to the boyfriend.

"It's too early to be certain. I . . . "

Then my bedroom door opened and a tall, dark figure stepped through.

I gasped, staring up from the floor, surrounded by my dolls spread all around the shoebox operating table in front of the bed.

The weary figure glared from the doorway, eyes narrowing, struggling with an arm-load of freshly cleaned clothes.

"Hi, Mom." I muttered, hanging my head. *Caught!* Caught *playing* with my toy collection. I could've died from embarrassment.

Mom huffed, stepping over the scattered, shattered remains of tonight's many ER patients. "Karen Sanders. What have I told you? If you don't stop wrecking your toys, they're going to wreck you!"

Wanna read something frightening? Something horrifying? Try reading . . .

SOMETHING ROTTEN

Enjoy this special, slithering sample but beware . . . it's oozing closer!

STRANGE MATTER™

#11 Something Rotten

by Marty M. Engle

1

"Hey, Joe! You just about finished? I want to go home!" my little brother whined, walking in a circle, staring at his size six sneakers as they kicked up a dry cloud of dust. Gary didn't like this field. It was too big. Too barren. Too dusty. Warm, spring days like today made the cracked, dry ground seem anxious for a cooling shower.

Gary spit, as if to comply with the ground's wishes, and kicked over a rock, the very goal of our expedition. Behind him, our suburban neighborhood stretched out in full view, spreading across the valley below.

"Got one!" I yelled excitedly, pulling the rock from the ground. "Feldspar Granite." At least that's what it looked like. Like most igneous rocks, granite is pretty easy to find. I turned the pinkish, speckled chunk over in my gloved hand as I raised it up, holding it against the bright blue sky. "A good one, too."

"Hoorah. Hurray. Let's go," Gary mumbled sarcastically, not even looking up.

"Could you at least fake interest for a moment?" I yelled, fumbling through the green canvas sack slung across my shoulder.

I slid it off and put it down on the ground in front of me, so I could find a specimen container more easily. "Do you even know what Feldspar Granite is?"

"It's what your head's made of," Gary sighed, bending over and picking up a pebble.

"You're a laugh riot, Gary. You need your own show on Fox or something. You, Hank and Darren could be the stars. Call it "Bratty Little Brothers" or something. A bold, fresh look at dorky siblings and the people they annoy."

"It'd come on right after "Skinny Joe Alister's World of the Weak," Gary laughed, cracking himself up.

"DON'T CALL ME THAT! You know I HATE that!" It's true. I'm skinny. *Way* skinny. Shrimpy even. Gary's the same way though, so he doesn't have a lot of room to talk. Our white t-shirts hang on us like sacks.

I growled, popping the lid off a rock container I fished from the canvas bag. It looked like a plastic jar that pills would come in. I plunked the chunk of rock inside and carefully wrote the date on the label.

I went rock collecting in the field after school, hoping it would cheer me up. Gary tagged along as usual, as if under contract.

We were both in lousy moods. I had been publicly humiliated at school that day, and Gary . . . well, Gary's always in a bad mood, unless he's in front of the TV.

"You know, I can't believe Shelly Miller actually *bench-pressed* you," Gary said.

"AWW, MAN! You think I wanna talk about that?" The bitter source of today's humiliation.

"Sorry, but straight up? Five times? Not even a strain, just . . ." Gary made a motion like a weight-lifter, pushing up a barbell from his chest.

"ALL RIGHT! ALL RIGHT, already! Enough! I don't want to talk about it," I cried.

David Donaldson and Shelly Miller got into a big fight about who was stronger and made a bet: who could bench-press *me* the most times? Actually the *Joe Alister-living barbell* part was Darren Donaldson's idea. Darren's flair for striking visuals and his friendship with Gary led to my involvement.

Absurd? Yes. Humiliating? Yes. But Shelly Miller sure is stronger than she looks.

Oh, they were nice about it, of course. They asked if I would do it, and like an idiot, *I agreed.* What could I do? Everyone was saying, "Please? C'mon. Be a pal. Be a sport. It's all in good fun, blah, blah, blah . . ."

How embarrassing. Still, I'm kind of used to it. Being the smallest kid at Fairfield Junior High is tough. Everyone looks down on me. Even Kyle Banner usually deems me unworthy of his barbaric attention.

"We've been out here for three hours. Can we go home now, please? There's this device in our living room called television that I need to sit in front of as much as possible." Gary's arm snapped up over his head and he flung something . . .

A small rock hit the ground right beside me and bounced up into my shin.

"HEY! Watch it! You could have hit me in the . . . hey, wait a minute. What was it you threw?" Gary wouldn't know a rare rock if he was holding it, *or* throwing it.

He watched me scour the ground and rolled his eyes in disbelief. "Oh man, give me a break! Excuse me, Sherlock, but it was just a stupid pebble! A nothing! A nobody among rocks. Just one of the ordinary, faceless sedimentary crowd."

I found it, popped it in a plastic jar and placed my new prize into the bag, another beauty to add to my growing collection. "These are igneous, not sedimentary, and there is no such thing as an ordinary rock. Every rock is different."

"Okay. I give up. I'm going back without you."

"Fine," I mumbled, bending over to check out a shiny, black pebble.

"I mean it!" Gary yelled.

"Great. Go. Bye."

He stopped. "Aw c'mon, Joe. Creature Features will be on soon. You want to see it, too. I know you do."

If they gave trophies for tantrum-throwing, nasally whines, or over-dramatic sympathy ploys, Gary wouldn't have an empty shelf. But this time, he was right. I wanted to see the show, too.

"All right. Let's go."

I took one last, long look out across

Fairfield, a thousand dots of light in a darkening valley. It sure looked nice from up here. The sun began to set and the sky turned a pinkish-purple.

"C'mon, Joe. It's a good one tonight, *The Blob!*"

THE SCARIEST PLACE IN CYBERSPACE.

Visit STRANGE MATTER™ on the
World Wide Web at
http://www.strangematter.com

for the latest news, fan club information,
contests, cool graphics,
strange downloads and more!

GET YOUR HANDS ON

Order now or take this page to your local bookstore!